MORTAL MORNING

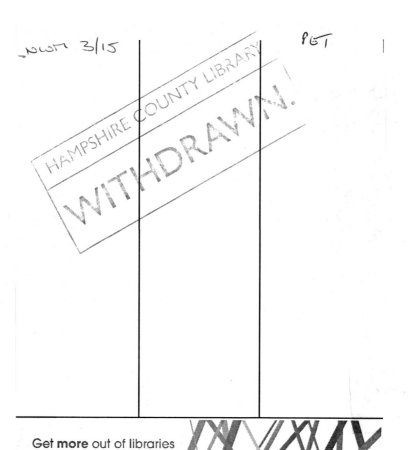

Get more out of libraries

Please return or renew this item by the last date shown.

You can renew online at www.hants.gov.uk/library

Or by phoning   0845 603 5631

Hampshire
County Council

MORTAL MORNING

Poems by

Brian Aldiss

FlambardPress

First published in Great Britain in 2011 by Flambard Press
Holy Jesus Hospital, City Road, Newcastle upon Tyne NE1 2AS
www.flambardpress.co.uk

Typeset by BookType
Cover Design by Gainford Design Associates
Front cover painting by Brian Aldiss
Printed in Great Britain by Bell & Bain, Glasgow, Scotland

A CIP catalogue record for this book is available from the British Library.

ISBN: 978-1-906601-21-8

Flambard Press wishes to thank Arts Council England
for its financial support.

Supported by
ARTS COUNCIL
ENGLAND

Flambard Press is a member of Inpress.

The paper used for this book is FSC accredited.

My love's name begins with an A.
What follows I must not say!
Not shy, not she, but private, yes.
This vexing darling also has a second name:
Here's an antimony to help you guess
Her surname, sirs, in this fair game.

Dear A, my dedication comes to this –
You're my late summer's solstice . . .

Acknowledgements

The following poems previously appeared in *At the Caligula Hotel* (Sinclair-Stevenson, 1995): 'At the Caligula Hotel', 'Breughel's Hunters in the Snow', 'Fernand Khnopff', 'Monemvasia', 'The Cat Improvement Company' and 'Flight 063'. Many of the other poems were published in *A Prehistory of Mind* (Mayapple Press, 2008), and are here reprinted with grateful thanks to wonderful Judith Kerman of Mayapple Press.

Contents

Introduction

The rest is
silence –
hence colour

I was always writing poetry, even as a boy, but more fervently now I am older. Similarly with my artwork.

Some of the artwork contains words. 'The psyche in search of itself' being an example. The two hemispheres of the brain collude in such a case.

Science declares that those two coral-like hemispheres which grow in the dark greenhouses of our skulls deal in one case with prose and numbers, and in the other case with colour and the pictorial. And, I suppose, with music.

But poems with their metaphors, their unexpected rhymes and rhythms – their unanticipated good sense – are they a bridge between these two vital vegetables?

The question slips in here, spies in the night, riddles in the mortal mornings. It has proved a profound joy, fashioning the somethings from something resembling nothing, with only the English tongue for guidance. Oh, and remembrances going back, of course, and crossing frontiers, going onward. Which arms, which is the other hemisphere?

Such dried petals and spices, this potpourri, has yet to yield its own answer. It's beyond me. You, too, slightly, I hope.

The Deceptive Truth

Digging deep in a Martian desert
Men discovered an enormous brain.
It suddenly started to think at them –
So they covered it up again.

A survivor said that a thunderstorm
Came bursting like a thing accursed.
A skeletal mathematical norm
Came rattling at them, then dispersed
Into enigmas and algorithms.
And what was hot was cold and cold was warm
And they were all immersed
In images that filled the skies
With superhuman enterprise –
Until he thought his head would burst.
The cold equations were the worst,
With insights sharp as tsetse flies.
'I couldn't tell the half of it,'
He said, before his final fit.

Did it know the Ultimate Truths
And see the All with unseeing eye?
Or were the chaps right, with their picks and drills,
In covering up an ultimate Lie?
Maybe it said how Life – *where* Life – began,
Upon a silent stone, light years from here,
How consciousness crept from a clutch of cells,
And what it is that seems to interfere
In the affairs of nations. Is a god
A fact or an illusion we all share?
Did the Brain say that on our Earth at least
Fish swim, birds fly, men sing, women are fair?

When confounded by mankind's ways
I think of the Martian temple wall
On which some bygone wag had scrawled
'Too much Truth will kill us all . . .'
Friends, forget the riddle Truth,
Tell the Ultimate to go away.
Perhaps the one great verity that matters
Is miraculous old Everyday.

Flight 063

Why always speak of Icarus's fall? –
That legendary plunge
Amid a shower of tallow
And feathers and the poor lad's
Sweat? And that little splash
Which caught the eye of Breughel
While the sun remained
Aloof within its private zone?

That fall remains
Suspended in the corporate mind.
Yet as our Boeing flies
High above the Arctic Circle
Into the Sun's eye, think –
Before the fall the flight was.
(So with Adam – just before
The Edenic Fall, he had
That first first taste of Eve.)

Dinner is served aboard Flight 063.
We eat from plastic trays, oblivious
To the stratosphere.

But Icarus – his cliff-top jump,
The leap of heart, the blue air scaled –
That first and foremost time –
His glorious sense of life
Imperilled. How the dull world
Fell far below, the everyday
Was lost in his ascent.

Up, up, he sailed, unheeding
Such silly limitations as
The melting point of wax.

The Moment

Passport? Yes. And boarding pass.
After a queue to dump one's luggage
Within the custody of powers unseen.
Crowds all with their own directions,
Polite up to a point. Our destinations
Differ, but mortality's the same,
Crossing all national boundaries.
Airports acknowledge this.
All these great stations to the need for travel
Are full of screens, instructions, bars,
Processing travellers to their planes
And various destinies.

Für Ihre Sicherheit –
      Und Our Convenience –
Stay belted in your seat.
We shall arrive
Upon a vapour trail of money.

This man has business deals in Frankfurt,
This woman goes to meet her sister
In Hong Kong. Some for business,
Some for love, will buy a place
High in the stratosphere.
                  This great commerce
Continues every day as world
Mingles with world and race with race,
Turban with tonsure, beard with ring-through-nose,
Sari with leather skirt.

Please have your boarding passes ready
For this moment in the human story.

The Kremlin, Moscow, Ca. 1950

This is the Terem Palace, visitor.
Survey it for five minutes.
Our Soviet scholars D. Sukhov
And N. Pomantsev have studied it
And written of its thorough pomp
Restored by recent architects.

You must note, firstly, the carved decor
Surrounding the portal as we enter.
The ribs of the fine vaulted ceiling
And the fretwork of the oak windowsills
Harmonise with the bright tiled stove.
The windows are latticed and thick with mosaic
That's seventeenth-century craftsmanship.
Too bad the weather is poor today.
So dark . . .
Bright murals are everywhere.
Among their baffling patterns are
Portraits of ancient saints.
This one is Theodore Stratelates –
Fourth century, put to death.
See how the chairs are gilded and embroidered.
Priests in Zagorsk embroidered them.
They're heavy to move.
Don't touch.
Remember as you look about
That this was once a sacred place.
Our coach waits in the square.
Now pass on quietly, visitor.
By the gold table yonder sits
Our Comrade Stalin, deep in thought.

Journeying

Ulan Bator, that red hero, lay four days
Behind us. We made but little progress
Eastward through the bare
Terrain. Occasionally a pool
Lay in the mighty palm of landscape.
There we drank, the horses drank,
We submerged ourselves in that glorious stuff.
For a whole day I thought about the miracle of wetness.

We entered more deeply into
The sovereignty of the steppes
Under the serious sky where we slept
Like lifeless bundles against the cold.
Waking, we smote ourselves to bring
Back life. A slow dawn etched a picture
Of the desolate grandeur
Surrounding us. I thought
All day of daylight.

Deep, we were deep into
The echoing immensity, the unpretty
China and the Moon
Which the great Khan once ruled.
And for a thousand miles there was
No road and nothing you might
Call a house. We journeyed on.
I thought of emptiness.

Now I am home, I shower
And dress and eat and switch
Off lights and lock my door.
The streets are bright and noisy,
Cars and coaches pass while
People flock into the nearest
Supermarket. So much to do and buy – and I
Think about myself.

Rapide des morts

The dead, we're told, all travel fast.
They speed in underground trains.
Their faces, pressed against the windows,
Show hollow-eyed anger at the stations
At which they never stopped.
      It's too late now . . .
They're aboard a non-stop express.
Nothing to do but stare buck-toothed
Out at the darkness. They've given up
Those pleasant living vices they once
Knew. They need no refreshment car,
No buffet, no clocks. They do not smoke or drink.
They moulder. As for love-making,
For which their flesh was made,
At least they never even think of it, no
Thought remaining in those glaucous skulls –

    Only a sullen fury
    That we live on
    And they did not
      Live enough.

Hiroshima Day, 6 August AD 2000

17

April in East Coker

Of course peace carries temptation.
You could live here amid these serious stones,
These leaded windows, the little stream with primroses,
The fatal quiet, the regular postal service.
You're miles from the nearest motorway
And the church still works. Nevertheless,
Isn't seeking old world peace a poor thing,
A poor thing to do? This place, its associations,
Beckon towards a falsehood,
Beckon us to a yesteryear not exactly ours –
Not really anyone's, not even the overseas visitor
Now resting eternally in the graveyard.

Better really to acknowledge there's no place
Any longer, no place that is not temporary
Or under threat. Tomorrow will be different
Except for what has fossilised or sleeps
Beneath these stones. Better really to face
The uncertainty beneath the veneer of things.
Better to realise that family problems are endemic
And that every government always lies.
Better to understand that most of what we know
Is handed down, contingent, untrustworthy.
Yet at the heart of things
Despite all our failings
Failings of dreadful kinds
Sins betrayals pretences
There forever remains
Something we must love
If we are to love anything
And thereby be of use:
Our perfect selves
Hidden inside imperfect circumstance.

Exmoor in September

These uplands have assumed the shape
Of a great marine leviathan
Stranded slumberous yet menacing
On the granite from which Devon grew.

Some holobathyic force abides
Nursing the crust of trilobite
Under Five Barrows surely lies
A vast marine thing beached in time
Dead ears tuned to raw primordial tides
Dead eyes still turned to Exmoor light
As if some forgotten ocean's bed
Had heaved itself into our ken
To clothe its rocks in grass and ling
For a disguise
Yet still remain beyond the grasp of men.

Once all the world was anthracite
Once all the air was fire and steam
Once all of day was night
But now – a realm where breath is.
Amphibious, I walk as in a dream
Under a sky as blue as Tethys.

The Cynar, Istanbul

An unknown hotel, night thoughts all slack
And lack of sleep about say 2 a.m.

Pulling back the curtains I step out.
Into a warm euphoria. All seems calm.
And there before my sight, unguessed, the moon
Full-faced gleams down upon the Sea of Marmora.

Tien Shan

Far in these Central Asian distances
The Tien Shan mountains rise
Over the horizon, untravelled like
A mighty grey planet. Animals roam
Free, indistinguishable in haze.
These solitudes I sought and found.
Oh, the air I breathed, with the unleavened
Bread beneath my saddle! And all
I could think of, heartsick, was
That years ago
In a distant city we two had loved
All through a summer month, and you –
My Monica! – I'll never know
Your tenderness
Your lips again.

Aral Seasons

When and if I find her
I can love her only till I die.
Best then to remind her
Even the deepest seas run dry.

Planners may plan to irrigate
A desert where the stony sand
Gives way at stroke of pen and hand
To figs and cotton. Profligate
With figures, men will then pretend
To yields on which careers depend.
Nature can gross – the planners say –
So many tonnes (one and x noughts)
In five years' time. Nature retorts
By raising pests in fierce array.

Luckily I found you
But I can love you only till I die.
Just keep my arms around you –
Even the deepest seas run dry.

The people strive, some cotton blooms,
Canals crawl wounded through the waste.
Vines grow. Grapes have a bitter taste.
Doubts startle in committee rooms.
Men glare at their computer screens,
To wonder what the bad news means.
Meanwhile, some hundred miles away,
The Aral Sea begins to die.
Love is not planned. So you and I
Enjoy our fruits as best we may,
And with contentment in our store,
Our ocean grows from shore to shore.

You won't need reminding
> I can love you only till I die.
> One day you'll be finding
>> Even the deepest seas run dry.

On Passing a Roadside Auction of Featherbeds

Lake District, 1845 (Courtesy of Harriet Martineau)

Wordsworth is growing old
And the great world too.
Not least this Rydal Mount
We are passing through.
The roadway needs repair:
Its ruts and boulders jar our heads.
But then we come upon
An old man selling featherbeds.
He is holding an auction of sorts
And from villages round
Or from farmsteads far apart
Come in crowds to cluster
About the man's cart:
A sandy-coloured crowd,
Many men in cords,
Some with the straggling white whiskers
Which labouring age affords,
Old women in bonnets,
A girl passing fair,
Tousle-headed children with puppies,
A youth leading a mare.
We pass, as the country folk
Jostle about, elbowing, eager to buy
The goods, old, newish, bespoke.
Thinking on this, our poet
Falls into gloomy meditation.
At least a new edition of his poems
Is in preparation.

Well, even in old age
We must fight our own battles.
The time draws nearer when
We won't need our goods and chattels.

Winter

In winter my mother's house is cold
Where she sits all day
To gaze at the Wo Lung River
Hardly dares to cough for dread of noise

Every day I mean to send her a letter
Why can we never say
The necessary words?
Why does frost draw such elaborate flowers
Upon the barrier of her window pane?

Of All the Places

Of all the places in the beleaguered world
But both of us were far from home
And how it rained – that monsoon rain
That made us run for shelter, laughing –
I hadn't planned to love you, yet
Perhaps I already did. I cannot read
My heart as easily as yours –
Or do I deceive myself –
Tell me, are you really the best and dearest
Woman on this planet – as I believe –
Oh, and in that restaurant, you said with your glass
Of Chardonnay – What was it we said –
What spell was cast so suddenly –
How am I still as one shell-shocked? –
We were in each others' arms – weren't we? –
And mouths, tongues, throats, bodies, interlocked –

Monemvasia

Reflections on a Greek theme

An ocean without motion lies before us
Like life itself of which we are an instance,
While fading headlands in an Attic chorus
Give out the antique news that tragic distance
Lies between reality and what's desired,
Until the heart toils and the eye grows tired.

We take some photographs and move on soon:
To prove that we were here who now are gone.
We have a date in Athens, Sunday noon.
'We made it!' Yes, but timetables roll on.
A tamarisk bends to the southern air
As calendars rule tourists everywhere.

And yet a secret self remaining free
Still stands like Monemvasia, above
The fray – a goddess who, to some degree,
Shows both insight and blindness, born of love.
While Greece itself withstands the blast,
Symbol of liberty, of what must last.

As here above the languid ocean's eye
Past builders built, layer on stony layer,
A fortress that would evermore defy
Invaders. Spite of cannonade and prayer
Dark, doughty enemies stormed the redoubt,
Refortifying, turn and turn about.

The day degenerates in coils of flame
To westward. Sea takes on its various hue,
Encouraging a mood I cannot name
With dreamy images I share with you.
All's calm, although breeze has its little tiffs.
We linger late upon the lonely cliffs

And watch the mighty shadow of this rock
Fall like a cloak upon the sea below,
Silent and sinister. These days we mock
Past ghosts, but many a sentry stood to know
The vengeful phantoms of a warrior state,
The pale precursors of blood, fire and fate,

Just as these olive trees emerge from rock,
Mesembryanthemum and herb from dry cliff face,
So, though our scenes are set where much is stock,
Something within us pines for unknown place,
For ruins which are immarcescible,
Springing from a time now inaccessible.

Evening! Sweet scents, and in the lower town
We wander many a weathered floral lane
Imagining as comely night comes down,
Venetian, Byzant, Frank, alive again
To scheme and dream as we do, for a spell.
Then we retire to our one-star hotel.

Much as we try to purify our days
Past traces wait within a footstep's fall;
We too are formed of what once was. Always,
The bird that chirps by yon *taverna* wall
Reprises time, wars, hopes and marjoram,
The Paleologues, Byron and Suleyman.

No more the brazen cannon airs its voice
For Monemvasia no more depends
On soldiery. At that we can rejoice.
Instead the tourists seek their various ends,
To photograph, to marvel, or to curse,
To picnic, or to improvise a verse.

If truly joy should be the aim of art
A visitor leaves here a better man.
If time had shaped this wreckage from the start
Is Ruin what an architect should plan? –
Just as some say our winter's evening
Is what we secretly desired in spring.

How comforting in this dull hour, to sleep
Among such ancient scenes, lulled by their peace.
The moon to the Aegean plunges deep;
The tumbled stonescapes of the Peloponnese
Imbibe her beams and, throughout summer's night,
Themselves reflect a dim historic light.

*

Many slow years have flowed since I was there
Leading my love about that solemn stone.
Now she has passed forever from my care!
My fair companion, my dearest own,
Haunts Monemvasia when daylight fades –
Her sweet young ghost amid the older shades.

I learnt one truth long since, when just a boy:
That happiness will ever claim its fee,
That sorrow adds its tint to every joy.
So as I sat high-perched above the sea
To write these lines, old ruined walls impressed
This traveller with the pain of being blessed.

The Heavy Cup

Beyond your curtained window
The autumn sun is up.
Your long fragile fingers
Scarcely clasp the breakfast cup.

Fine porcelain is weighty for you,
Your tea has lost its taste.
All things once lovely in your presence
      Run to waste.

Set down the cup, close those tired eyes.
Sleep, my sweet! I too will fade
And our life together, like
This direful day, be but a shade.

Spinal Metaphors

The little bones of my lover's spine
Are as delicate as knitting needles
Blunt enough to be kissed.
They grow more marked when she is dying –
When you both stay silent with your fears –
More like the knuckles of a clenched fist.
        Death has much to teach
By way of beauty, loss, and tears.
The skin, light as a summer's shower
And as uncertain, slowly retreats
Leaving behind a trail of pebbles
        On a dying beach.
All of these metaphors are very fine
But do not cure my lady's spine.

Comfort Me, Sweetheart

'Oh, comfort me, sweetheart,
My years are behind me.
For I am now going
Where no man can find me.'

    I gave my love a casket of silver
    With its velvet lining showing.
    'Place my heart in this, my darling,
    Take it with you where you are going.'

'Oh, the way's long and dreary
To go down the mountain.
There's no place to rest me,
No lodging or fountain.'

    I gave my love a flask of chaste crystal
    Like a pure snow cloud snowing.
    'Place my blood in this, my darling.
    Take it with you where you are going.'

'Oh, I fear for my journey
And the ills that now ail me,
With no one to ward off
The frosts that assail me.'

    I gave my love the breath of my body
    Like the warm south wind blowing.
    'Wrap this round you, my darling,
    To cloak you well where you are going.'

Oh gone is my lover, whose arms once entwined me,
Her light leads me onwards upon that same highway.
    Alone I make my way
To meet her and greet her, my years all behind me.

Get Out of My Life

Get out of my life –
I'm worn out with giving
With sharing and caring, with hoping and crying
And fearing your leaving.
Since I can't bear to be living
With all I love dying,
Just leave me to grieving.

Get out of my life,
You dear precious treasure!
No more let pain rack you and ravage
Your frail constitution.
Bereft beyond measure
I'll drink then the savage
Wide world's destitution.

Being a Little Well

Couldn't you be a little well
  For a little while longer?
Oh how I love your presence
  And your virtue
If you could be just a little stronger
  Would that hurt you?

All fair things perish, we know,
Yet death is a horrid surprise –
  Just to see you so low
It rips my heart in two.
Tears burst unprompted from my eyes
  Is there nothing I can do?

No, there's nothing I can do.
  Just for a little while
Be a little well, love, if you can
  Grant me that lovely smile.
I promise I'll smile too.
As I hold your frail hand, I'll
Hold back the chill that will befall.
Can't you be a little well at all?

This Brown Leaf

I give you this brown leaf to keep.
      It's one of many.
      It fell away
Too early from its tree.
Hold it, love, while you sleep,
This token of the transience of things,
Sleep through this fine still day,
While our world runs to seed.
You should be waking, walking,
      Smiling your dear smile
That blessed my many springs.
      Now – well, it's autumn indeed
For our love, for you.
      Seems our days are almost done.
      What can I do?
This leaf has thousands like it.
      Like you there are none, none.

Leaving Our Common Bed

Leaving our common bed
In which my dying darling lay,
I dreamed I crept downstairs
Barefoot and in some dread.
In the obscuring fog I sensed
The floor below was filled
With a great oily sea,
Black and with strange turbulence.
Pausing upon a step I felt
The waters climb about my toes.
What monsters dwelt
Within the flood I did not know.
As I withdrew my foot, a hand
Was raised up from the tide.
'Who's there?' I cried –
And then I saw a corpse
Half-flooded, half-afloat.
I took its hand and found
It cold and bloated.
I dragged it on to firmer ground
Among mixed shingles on the shore
And boats with broken staves.
People were there, ignoring me.
Looking at the dead man I could see
He had my hair, my looks.
I had myself been lost below the waves.

Rest Your Weary Head Upon Your Pillow

Rest your weary head upon your pillow
     Try to regain some ease.
While you're within my care I'll serve and love you
And lift the glass of water to your lips
I kissed so passionately long ago.
Let me suffer with your suffering, please,
And die with you each day as living slips
Further into the chill zone of Co-proxamol,
Bendrofluazide, and Domperidone.

Rest your weary head upon your pillow
     Try to retain some strength.
I'm with you and will wash and iron your garments
And smile back to that gently smiling face
I read with all concern. Minutes and seasons
Slip away – and each of lesser length:
Curtains more drawn, footfalls more soft to place.
'Are you awake, love?' Bless the hours when she
However faintly gives the answer, Yes . . .

Margaret's Questions

I'm cold here and it's dark.
What's happening?
    Will this peace
    Never cease?
Do dogs still bark?
Do birds still sing
As once they did
In the pure clear air
When I was there
And death lay hid?

Was I not beautiful then
And delightful to kiss?
Did I not please him when
We shared so much bliss?

It's dark here and I'm cold.
Why can't I move?
    Why is my mind
    Consigned
To wretched mould?
He whom I love –
But no longer touch –
Does he still groan
And sleep alone
And miss me much?

A House on the Island of Poros

Supposing that you bought a house on Poros
Leaving English things behind,
Would not much of English happiness
Come flooding back to mind?
Supposing that you learnt a little Greek
To buy some items at the store,
Would not the text of *Hamlet* wreck your heart
And draw you home once more?

But, after all, the good simplicity
Of two rooms and a kitchen touch
A chord. The whitewashed cottage by the shore
Would satisfy so much
That one would read the old philosophers
And then, forgetting England, take
A dark-eyed woman to your table and
Your bed, for loving's sake.

And in a small *taverna* by the beach
With draft *retsina* in your glass,
You'd talk of distant wars with pleasant friends
And laugh. The days would pass
With swimming naked in the warm blue Gulf,
Evenings with films or books or song,
Night-times full of sweet fulfilling sleep
Where old dreams belong.

But stop! – All this is nothing but a wish.
Engendered by a summer's grey
And English lid of sky. That Poros house
Is far too far away
For reason's reach. In truth there's no escape
From circumstance at this late stage
In life. The house is neither bought nor built.

Nea Kameni at Dawn

Into the secrets of our parents' lives
We soon inject the question, *Who am I?*
And who are you? Why don't you say?
See the light flashes
And indifferently the questions die.

For we too have our day.
Mischief, enquiry and clean shirts,
Some girl sweet-smelling in a bed –
Those early years soon blown away.

Our parents' generations held notions
Later proved wrong and out of date.

Most of the poor devils were celibate.
They could not credit continents and oceans
Can move, and some believed the Moon
– Accustomed as they were to wrecks –
Child of a great volcanic parturition.
Ejected from its parent Earth, y'know,
From the wide Pacific womb below.

This was their way of talking sex.
Think of it then! Now science has taught us
Not only more about the cosmos
But how to bring up learned sons and –
Excuse the vile rhyme – daughters.

Okay. Let's have the nitty-gritty.
This island's called Nea Kameni.
The Greeks have a way with language, right?
Nea Kameni. Not at all pretty.
A lowly crust where nothing grows,
Another moon where lift-off never struck.
      Darlene and I will camp here for the night.
            She will sleep and I shall doze.

So daughter and I jump from the boat
To pick our way with caution up the slope.
We pitch our bivouacs (brand new!), so glad
That tourists avoid tavernless spots like these.
Darlene is my adored. When Maud and I broke up,
She didn't give two hoots.
I taught her to love the world abroad. To think! –
She's my firstborn and now she works in Boots!

We hardened travellers can cope
With hardship when there's seascape to be had,
As here, of blue Aegean, setting sun, with Santorini's cusp
And distantly, lights of the basking Cyclades.

'Goodnight, my pet.' She answers me.
Sleep comes to her much like a docile hound;
But not to me, however hard I strive.
Her gentle breathing makes a soothing sound.
Below our blankets, lava, pumice, dust,
Fall-out from some passing asteroid,
Discarded, unrevived,
Since this gob of land was thrust
Out of a boiling eighteenth-century sea
Out of the spewing magma, just a haemorrhoid,
Its weals, its woe, settled here long ago.

I rouse to sunlight and the smell
Of coffee. Darlene tends the stove,
To greet me with a word and gleaming look
And soon a steaming cup as well.
'You lazy old pop,' she says. 'Get up!
I've had a swim already.' She takes up her book.
I drink and then at last succeeding
To achieve the vertical. And yawning still, I gape
About us. 'It's a Max Ernst lunarscape,'
I say, smart-arsed. She nods but goes on reading.

The boat pulls in below and 'Here's our man!'
I tell her, and she rolls her bedding up with some disdain.
I take her arm to guide her to the tiny shore.
To the boatman she's polite, but nothing more,
Playing the prim recusant.
I see she's taking up her book again.
The water's green and clear
– What else can you say of it? – translucent.

As the coast comes near
And wavelets dance
Like lucky bookies
I ask as nicely as I can
If by any chance
She'll tell me
What her book is.

She just says, 'Isfahan.'
'You're quite wrapped up in it.'
She gives me an irritated glance.
'Tamerlane is such a shit.'

Within the bounds of air and earth and sea
Our human lives must make the best of what must be
Aware that something baffling always runs
Even between our daughters and our sons.
Just a glimpse of light
Like windows glittering on bonfire night.

See How She Dances

See how she prances,
Pirouettes, dances.
Limbs flashing, eye lashing,
Dashing.
Youth and energy in collusion,
Clashing.
Beautiful with legs so long,
Profusion
Within a heart so light, so strong.

In the Houses of Parliament,
Where law for once met sentiment,
They passed an Act of Agelessness
And quelled an ancient argument:

Here's death to an ancient Adversary!

Bright as a berry, inexhaustibly merry,
Well may she dance! See how she dances! –
New legislation in promulgation
Makes her caper. Oh, the glad sensation!
No more old age . . . No pills required –
Physicians all fired –
Musicians are hired!
Only that long, long desired
Dear youthfulness forever!

Limbs fail her never
Through fitness, through chances
Through sunlight's glad glances
Life forever enhances –
Enhances forever!

See how she dances!

That Nameless Scent

Quiet now! Can't you smell that scent
Pervading all your senses –
For everything the same –
From here into the Oort Cloud?

How strange that it should have no name
Since it is in all matter, everything
That has ever been on earth
That came or was indigenous
That is or was existing
From mountains to the smallest pebble –
Insect, animal or plant insisting
That it must be. There's that elusive
Scent, pervasive, till a grand conclusion
Closes the whole vast drama down.
A perfume of existence with no name –
Even a name like evolution.

Greed

Mourning has no nobility. It's a hunger,
A sort of animal, always unexpected.
It leaps out when you're unawares.
There's the sound of the gate, perhaps,
Or you find an old postcard signed
'With love.' Or her dresses are glimpsed
Hanging in the spare wardrobe.
Almost anything's enough, and once again
Your loss comes in a flood. It's not
Nobility. It's barely love. It's just the sense
That nothing good or beautiful can ever
Happen again without her. That your life,
Much like her own, has ceased. It's not
Greed either, just a wish to glimpse even her
Shadow, to feel her turning in the bed
In sleep, to touch again her slender
Hand, to have her for a day, an hour
And pour out all your love and grief.
Oh no, that's greed all right, it's wishing
Desperately for the impossible.

The First of March 1998

Days? One hundred and sixteen
Days have passed
– Slow as time has ever been –
Since I saw her last.

And one hundred and sixteen nights
Grey as a northern sea
Since all delights
Were closed to me.

Sixteen weeks just over
Have wretchedly unfurled
Their wrappings since my lover
Left this world.

Weeks, months – how they extend!
Yet this 'I' survives
Long after the end
Of our joint lives.

Jocasta

Son sleeping with mother
And mother with son
Hot under the covers
Long into the Thracian night.

Different times, different manners,
We say, feeling strangely involved
In lust, perversion, tenderness,
Under their pseudonym of 'Love'.
The bedbugs could have warned them
Nemesis was on its way –
Those heavy footsteps in the mind.
Dark deeds of yesteryear, to burst
Like buboes, bringing sorrow,
Exile, blindness, death to the family.
But a desire so strong! – It made of them
A legend down the centuries.

Caught up in a machinery
Even geneticists can't explain –
As we too are inexplicable.

Lu Tai

Of course I could tell you of Lu Tai
Who hates to go to bed alone.
She is not the cleverest or the fairest
     And her little dog roots up my salvias;
But ah, when Lu Tai has her limbs about you
It could rain cucumbers for all I care.
For the sake of Lu Tai's golden kisses
     The young Buddha would forswear archery.

Antigone's Song

Who knows where my thoughts may lead me?
Does the rose that climbs my wall
And buds and flowers, heed me at all
As it rambles outwards, quite uncaring
While successive daylights run
For aught except the rain and sun?

I know not where my thoughts may lead:
All day they're ever onward faring,
Inconclusive, never done:
Dreaming blossom, dreaming seed,
As if, within my idle brain,
The very roses of my soul,
They generate their sun and rain –
In gardens free of my control.

Who knows where my thoughts may lead me
Or what hopes they may uncover
As the stormy clouds unroll?
Will I find someone to need me,
Will I find a perfect lover –
Perfect love to make me whole?

A Piece of Cleopatra

The centurion stands at attention
Watching Antony, who fidgets
Impatient to be kept waiting.

Finally Cleopatra comes
Barefoot, escorted by her maids
Who wave fans of ostrich feathers.

Her scent wafts to the soldier's nose
The rustle of her silks to his ears
Her subtle figure to his eyes.

He sees through her thin silk dress
To a dark triangle of hair.
Then Antony dismisses him.

Colour Contrasts

Frost and its crackling silences.
The dead of night. The general rests
His huge raw fists upon a dossier.
On his table burns an oil lamp
Giving forth a golden glow.
Beyond tall curtainless windows
Snow lies. Bright moonlight floods the room
Its silver vanquishing the gold.
Footsteps break the stillness, boots
On stone. Four soldiers hustle in
A prisoner. He's made to stand
Before the general. His blood
Drips richly on the bone-white floor
Dark as molasses.

Mortal Morning

All things are dual, such as night and day.
The morning is as mortal as the men it serves.
It creeps into the world like a straight line
Which slowly takes on colour. Amid clouds
It grows into uncertain adolescence
To be a cheerful day or sullen one.
Whatever is its mood a man must work,
Knowing full well dawn has a darker brother.
Sunset will surely drag its sister down
Into the oceans and the realms of night –
As we without intending bear our parents down
To somewhere that the sun can never light.
We all form part of great material worlds
Are one with hills and birds and leaves.
From this subservience, spirit's born
Which singing gives as it receives.

The Prehistory of the Mind

Shivering
Grunting to himself
Carrying a favourite stick
Stumbling along the arid beach
Hoping to find a fish trapped in a pool
Knowing the sun in its boat was sinking
Leading two ill-fed women and a meagre child
Feeling the thud of waves upon the shell-strewn sand
Fearing the night might catch them hungry and unprepared
He stubbed his toe upon a stone.

Picking it up, he found it pale and round.
The moon low in the sky was round and pale.
He looked from moon to stone and back
And back again as if to doubt his eye
Standing transfixed while sun sank under
Sea. His soul rejoiced in wonder
Without his knowing why.

Volcano

He shrouded himself in fume and smoke,
Rumbled and grumbled, and then he spoke:

I'm a volcano. I admit
My outpourings can cause distress.
No one likes what I produce –
But what's a village more or less?

Think of this: when I was done
Peasants came back and repossessed
The land. Those emblems of my fire,
That ash, is where the vine grows best.

I'm no psychologist, of course,
But this is where the Fertile starts –
Eruptions! Those draw Meaning best
Who draw dark matter from their hearts.

He ceased, and drew a turbid cloak
About himself of fume and smoke.

At a Base on Ganymede

Ridge after ridge confounds the weary sight
More desolate than eye could ever know,
Without fertility, yet roughly turned
As if by some mad ploughman long ago.

Yet to this arid site we gladly came
To find and see what we could see and find.
However bleak, however much it cost,
Compelled by something in the Western mind.

Just as in ancient days those cockleshells
Set out from Thames and Tiber, other sorts
Of vessel have now launched upon a sea
More fearsome far, for far more fearsome ports

Where there was neither oxygen nor wood
Nor living creature, till we humans came –
The ancestors, who give this moon its life,
Of those who once gave Ganymede its name.

Who would not long to find this distant port?
To watch, like moonrise over Africa,
The night be stormed – as from the barrens looms
Great Jupiter, a gross and golden star?

We cannot rest, for resting means decline.
The old Renaissance and the news it brings
Spurs us to daring, distance, deeds, and on
To conquer vast new unimagined things.

Perspectives

The monk shouts to a passing tank, 'It's all gone wrong!'
Churches are filling up with wounded people
Lacking arms or hands or eyes
While machines stand idle by Egyptian tombs.
A mine explodes. A peasant's leg goes flying.
A woman begins a wailing song.
Her malformed baby is crying, covered in shit and flies.
Nearby is a mass grave: a foot or two is showing
Above the soil. There's a drought, or a flood, or it's snowing.
Or something like that.

They say that in some nameless region
Earthquakes have claimed a thousand souls.
And there – or is it somewhere else? –
Dysentery and cholera are legion.
Of course, we always knew as much.
In doorways where the homeless beggars dossed
They died of cold. But heat has claimed its clutch
Of victims in Zaire. A Swiss airbus
Has crashed: all passengers lost;
Their bodies distributed
Over several miles of forest –
The generosity of the dead.

History strikes the old republics of the East.
Where did the human race go wrong?
Soldiers do what soldiers have to do.
Killing for a song, inadequately policed.
A bald-headed child holds out an empty mug.
     Disturbed by all this?
                  Not in the least.

The Bonfire of Time

The Eternal Spirit made a great bonfire of time,
Prancing round it, screaming, to see it blaze.
A whole continuum turned to soot.
In an almighty flue. The biomass – everything of flesh and slime –
All the biological things which consumed oxygen –
Went upwards, flashing, like a waterfall in reverse
Spewing up their years and months and days.
The molecules of which the galaxy was made
Boiled and popped like quark-flavoured nuclear lemonade.

Nebulae became mere sparks. In branch and trunk and root
Sequoias and great trees cried with the shrieks of burning men
As they were barbecued back into spore and seed.
Strata of rock, igneous and otherwise – ha, mere burnt paper,
    brittle!
Mountains and worlds, planets – those pearls of the universe –
Went up in the temporal smoke. Suns were never seen again.
Hissing out in a thin line of spittle,
The noise much like that of a beaten tin drum.
All those iconic intricacies that life and bloodstream made
Consumed to annihilation in that senseless Centigrade.

The Spirit himself, made mad by his own eternal curse,
Plunged to immolation. Such was the effect of this cosmic deed,
That even in the parallel universe next door –
Yes, even in the remotest comet's lair –
Cosmology itself was singed, and Kingdom Come
Rattled the inhabitants with its eschatological roar.
The inhabitants at once invented prayer.
Since your love and mine ignited, we have made,
I pray, a conflagration fit for heaven's fire brigade.

Iceberg Music

Compose me some iceberg music please
With groaning saxophones, shrill piccolos
And the dull throb of a leather gong.

It will help my life to freeze,
As when Greenland sends its floes
With fog and cold on currents strong

Enough to feed the shipping lanes
With pack-ice from mid-sea to shore.
As long as the iceberg music plays

The frost within my heart remains
Bitter as winds from Labrador,
Blasting the Arctic of my days.

'Midnight in Moscow' says the song.
The broken pavements of our lives
Help midnight's music move along.

Jackie

Sitting there at the next table –
    This was a busy Friday
        At the railway station –
A woman with a neglected cup of tea.
I thought, 'There's a sad woman.
    Sad and discontented.'
Her face was worn and thin –
    'Much like her clothes,' I thought.
Her husband joined her, looking tired.
    Did I know his face?
He smoothed a builder's plan upon the table
And wearily they disagreed about it.

    Well, I read my paper
        Checked my watch
            Drank my cappuccino
Till unexpectedly the woman spoke my name.
We got to talking with some pleasure.
    They lived out of town
        They had a bungalow
    Her parents both were dead –
Father died twelve years ago
    'Mother never recovered from his death.'

I'd known her when she was a little girl
A welcome playmate for our Clive
    Bright, well-mannered, full of promise
        She used to dance in our front room.
Now she teaches drama somewhere-or-other –
    'Yes, I enjoy it very much.'
        She's being brave. He smiles as well,
    Glad perhaps to hear her talking lightly.
Her smile reaches across to me
    Across the years that have made us
        Unrecognisable to each another
    Outwardly and inwardly.

The Women

The women gather every morning
Outside the supermarket
To smoke and chat. Their conversation
Is compounded of identical expressions,
Identical idioms, identical complaints.
They laugh with similar brief notes of grievance.
Their vocal inflections do not change
Whether they talk about ovarian cancer
Or the rise in price of Marmite.
For them, all such phenomena
Have an equally incomprehensible origin:
Disaster is always imminent,
Privation lies permanently in wait,
Health service is no good these days,
Men are always the oppressors,
And kids a burden.
They worship God, they say,
And often vote Conservative
Just out of desperation.
They're that good-hearted
But they've always been hard-done-by
And all agree
Life isn't what it was.

Uzbecks in London

In a season of cold weather
Women talk of Samarkand
And the Fulham bus.
Their menfolk congregate together
Holding children by the hand
Looking much like us.

> They have come from Central Asia
> To gather in the Conway Hall
> And make a little music.

> We seek at first for what's familiar
> To the sense most kin to sound
> Coiled among what's strange.

Then Munojothon enters and stands
Hand upon breast in greeting.
Eyes dark from orient south,
Behind her, *gijak* with its turkey neck,
Santar with its many strings,
And *tablar* with its fingered thud,
Serve as a river whereupon her voice
Floats. Sound streams from that regal mouth
As hair grows painlessly through skin
Or dawn ignites the desert sand.
The audience embarks upon that flood.

> Somewhere East of Caspian we navigate
> The winding flow of alien tongue
> From that pale ineffable throat
> And seek to find the meaning
> Fresh on those red lips.

The Bare Facts

She phoned me in delight one week,
Saying the child within her womb
Was six weeks old. 'It measures now
Almost a centimetre!' – She from Athens.
They had listened to its heart beat.

Then in its seventh week the husband phoned.
Something to do with chromosomes:
It failed within its crimson nest.
She'd known there was something wrong:
There was no heartbeat.

Could it be dead which had not lived?
Not quite a baby, more a possibility,
A hope, a chance of difference
For parents and the family. But no
Illusion. They had heard its heart beat.

Nor could there be a burial. It had
No name, no sex. The knitting of bootees
Had not begun. I though to make a poem
Of this mystery. But pain and longing bar
All but the record of bare facts:
Its heart had ceased to beat.

Nocturne

Borges could not decide whether this world
was realism or fantasy. Or perhaps he was
just playing with words. But who would be
daring to play with Borges?
I dislike the word *fantasy*, and most
of the stuff bearing that name: the
dragon thing or people trudging
back from the dead; it all
seems to defy rationality.
Yet realism with its rainy streets
also holds falsity. Look,
this is what I like
and this is how I live –
And even Borges cannot
decide upon a name for it.

I hear the dreamy music
Of this closing day.
How much I love my life
How mysterious my stay.

Fairy Tales

Here stand I in this desolate last resort
Close by the pier, the urinal, and a shuttered chipper
I know why Cinderella fled and lost her slipper
Too timid to show any love of any sort

It's easy to understand how adulthood
Lives out a fairy tale so far from pure
Like the pier knee-deep in chill seawater you're
A babe still searching for a decent wood

It doesn't always end as we might wish
With pots of gold at rainbow's base
Instead you may run up against an ogre's face
A mad axeman, an oven, or a bloody head upon a dish

The Cat Improvement Company

We founded the Cat Improvement Co.
For the betterment of the feline kind.
While taking their happiness to heart
We also had human good in mind.

As the blueprints show, all those spiky teeth
Were requiring removal from tiny jaws.
To improve the symmetry of the whole
We decided against the whiskers and claws.

The morality too of the average cat
Could be certainly optimised straight away
By unwinding the helix of Felix's genes
And blotting out some DNA.

The result is a quadruped bound to please,
All buttery soft and cushiony nice:
It pays no attention to moths or birds.
It has an abhorrence for catching mice.

Moreover, the Cat Improvement Co.
Gives with each pet a guarantee:
'Outside bedroom windows it will not yowl;
Also in corners it will not pee.'

Ceaseless research moves forward yet
As we tackle the troublesome question of eyes.
What shall be done to stop that glare
At spaces nothing occupies?

The CIC agenda shows
Updating is needed on silkier fur,
On gluttony, laziness, slinking,
And that aggravating purr.

The Perfect Cat is our ultimate aim
While, as far as technology reaches,
The HIC too is fulfilling its norms,
Improving the human species.

The New Philosophy

Time sprang into existence
But where exactly did existence come
From? Could existence be some theorised thing:
But comprehensible – cause and effect perhaps
Or distance and velocity, as Hubble
May have said.

'Nothing' has no properties
And no, we may not ask what came before
Existence, for 'before' is just a part of speech.
It has no role in an expanding universe
And there again maybe eternal expansion takes the stage.
It's an hypothesis, one with the multiverse.
Black holes spawn other universes
Like ours or not.

Besides, there was a previous universe
As generous with its stars as we with ours.
The theory is it shrank to – may I say
Pint-size? – only to re-arise
Refreshed and stocked with galaxies
Like ours, we think.

We really need a new mathematics
Uniting Einstein and the quantum theory.
Then we may perceive that time's
A contradiction born of gravity as now
Revealed by several learned scientific minds
In Canada.

Our mouths were well designed
To take in meat – the flesh of mammoths, say.
Have they now advanced so greatly
They can give out unspeakable truths?

The Foot Speaks

Sir, I am your humble foot:
I venture now to speak
Not only for myself
But for my silent twin,
To crave your good attention,
To ask why you imprison me –
Me and my delicate deft toes –
Each day within your shoe.
Only at night do you release us.
I never see daylight
And the sun.
The day you learnt to tread on me,
When I was young and tender,
You gained new powers and power
Over me.
Why do you, depending on me, shun me,
Never think of me,
Never give me a glance?
Have I not served you well?
I am your humble foot, sir,
Your unacknowledged footman,
Meet only for chiropodists.

Andrei Rublyev

It's told that you saw goodness with the eyes of reason.
In the late fourteenth century when you were born.
Great works of art like yours lasted but a season.
The well-horsed Ottoman was making his incursions.
Only in monasteries did culture not meet scorn,
Or sorrowing hold nothing intellectual.
And there, five hundred years ago,
'The Holy Trinity' was wrought.
In innocence and just proportions,
As if such holy good could reign perpetual.
The angels sit in meditation slow
To dream humility will bring a golden state
To dream in gold leaf of a realm of nought
But God and goodness. Oh, so very long ago!

The centuries go by in sullen chains
And fade. Still, still, the vintage dream remains.

Men and women die, while tyrannies abate
And even empires prove stramineous,
Yet something of the spiritual at least lives on.
So that in the Sixties of a later date,
Andrei Tarkovsky shoots a film whereon
He mates his moody genius with genius;
And 'Rubylev' is thus revived through dolour,
Through mist and murk – and sometimes brilliant colour –
His art and sanctity triumphing over death and squalor.

Breughel's Hunters in the Snow

The freeze continues. There's little to put in the pot.
They don't speak. An hour more and darkness will fall.

They're weary, and made all the wearier
By their lack of success.
Perhaps they'll have a drink at the inn
Before trudging home to confess
It's going to be bread and salt again.
Winter's not much of a time.

Father was never one to complain.
Once he was past his prime
He merely became unsociable
As if he was one of the hunters in the snow.
He'd say when we went out anywhere,
'Let's hope we don't meet anyone we know' –
As though a word might give him away.
Mother became pretty silent too.
When you come home empty-handed
You'd keep your trap shut, wouldn't you?

G B Tiepolo

A leprous dream world makes a curtsey
in Giambattista's *scherzi*

The wider world has disappeared
A serpent smoulders on an altar
A priest both over-dressed and weird
Offers a chant up to an unknown god
From paths where naked women trod
With many a fear and falter.

Satyrs and astrologers, goat-faced,
As smoke billows from the ruins
(For here all's ruined), taste
Philosophies of misery or joy.
It's none too pleasant.
Monkeys, owls, and scraggy dogs abound.
A bearded Oriental peasant
Sits on the ground with wife and boy,
While slabs of marble, richly carved, remain
Half-buried, lost from Rome's long reign.

Dusk gathers behind the tattered palms
The sun at best a pallid yellow
Here a snake, a mangy bird
And Punchinello, newly disinterred,
Against a boulder leaning
Is calculating numerous harms.

Of all this picturesque, what is its meaning?
What lurks untold?
Explain it? – No one can,
Held in the wrinkled palm of vision of an old
Beloved artist and man.

Caspar David Friedrich

Looking from my Eastern windows early
I watch the bars of chilly grey and blue
Before a brighter colour intervenes
To indicate a slowly rising sun.
It's then I'll think with Caspar David's mind,
As the stale domestic scenes are lit
And stale domestic tropes begun.

Humanity and light . . . a man with coat,
His back to us, is seeking for a scene
Of sombre spirit lit with holiness.
Mountains, snow and broken ships afloat
On ice must stand for purity delayed . . .

The touch, like snow, is light and smooth and soft.
So we are confronted every day
Within our world of flesh, and are afraid.
Friedrich turns to the Cross to paint and pray.
I turn away, sorry I scoffed,
Knowing something eternal has decayed.
My hat is doffed,
And I'm alone, no God aloft!

John Martin

The Brontë sisters in their vicarage beds
Would cower beneath your latest masterpiece,
Awed by your dreadful vision of the Flood
Perhaps. As I have often felt compelled
To seek Belshazzar at his mighty feast,
In his great chamber, infinitely long
But airless. Airless Pandemonium,
Too, throws up an architectural
Cityscape of Hell, where Satan stands,
Immaculate in Evil. These great piles
You build from otherwise unknown red stone –
Jurassic stone? – in which to house the damned,
No comfort there . . . The Bible and high-fly-
ing verse from Milton; from these come your props:
Your angels ride the hurricane of death
Into a light the Book illuminates –
The Book a melodrama of your whim . . .

When Gideon Mantell appears with all
His facts and fancies from geology,
The fossils of the iguanadon
Are given substance by your art –
As in your frontispiece to Mantell's book,
Wherein the loathsome reptiles of the past
Devour each other. Darwin's book was soon
To come – and redirect the Western kind
To live beneath a chillier moon,
To seek another cooler way to think:
Your grandiose and worked-on work would sink
Into its grave, however lush, while you,
Forever blind, will clutch
Your Bible and your fevered brush
To leave its trace upon the human mind . . .

Fernand Khnopff

You will recall the unruly beating
Of the heart in your throat, with breath constricted,
That something more than love you bore your sister.
Your ghostly images of something less than happiness,
Dreams, silence, hair, the scents of *femmes fatales,*
Burne-Jones and Schopenhauer and Socialism.
The century crumbling to its end. Stale cake.

When wandering through Bruges the other day
I saw the dead city through your dead eyes.
Despite the ice-cream parlours
Bruges-la-Morte among its old canals
Still drowns in your reflections.

What charcoal and pencil once created
Proves more powerful than stone.
The god of sleep who held you by the hand
In *timor mortis* seeks to find
How I contrived a freer life.

My Heart does not Cry for the Past
I relish all your symbolism
Closed interiors and leopard with a girlish face.
Yet I do not – nor ever can –
I Lock My Door upon Myself

It's your skill to mystify
Surround your self with negatives
And portray perverse images.

Remember the stale mornings and the mists.
Sappho in half-completed pastel,
Waistcoats, shadows, opium
And the shuttered bedroom windows.

Oh yes, and the canals
winding to who knows where.

Gauguin's Tahiti

As a kingfisher flashed from the lagoon,
Cynar splashed along the foreshore in the evening tide,
        And all its wild sky ride
Swaggered with atmospheric blues and greens.
Sunset, as no man else had dared to conjure,
Swallowed a new-born moon, and rolled towards the hut
        Wherein that great nude slut
Stared at occultly decorated screens

Behind the bed. Whereon, as on the screens,
Her man lay drugged, body turned olive like the night.
        Upon the woman's right
Her beaten bronze bowl stood stacked high with fruit,
Fruit that waxed luminous as flesh decayed,
Fish-fruit, fox-fruit, to make your lips curl back afraid –
        Fruit like a fear delayed –
Yet in dreams densely denizened the brute

Abed had gorged himself upon her flesh.
The painter cruelly caught them just before they died:
        The sunset in its pride,
The man in lechery, and in the room
Viridians of evil. So the seer
Inside the poet and the devil in the saint
        Achieve the power to paint
Invisible but all-encroaching doom,
To warn and warn that one night, all we've been
Will be the dust of nothing, and what life we saw
        But patterns on a screen.

To warn and warn that one night, never more –
As in the drownings of a fevered dream –
To light and warm us, down will sink the lurid sun
        Beneath its seas, and none
Will see us more upon this passionate shore.

Kandinsky

Take the 'singing of the colours':
the distinction lies between
say Neapolitan yellow
and emerald green.

Discrete chromatic spheres
mean that certain harmonies
appear only in the course of time.
This is where your genius is.

Quite early on, your landscape with church
tends to dissolve into yellows and blue.
Russian beauties, human beings, street scenes
will all fade in your search
when colours break free
to construct something New.

Structuralism is not only intellect
or what it may precisely seem.
There is formality – but less reality.
What is life without extremes?

Could I have lived without your work?
Possibly, to some extent.
Yet you have greatly fed my consciousness
to inculcate my grave consent
and fill my mind's sails with your argument.

di Chirico

An echo in a lonely street
Iron sky bereft of cloud
Tinkle of compasses
Whistle of departing train
Things without hands or feet
Crying of loneliness aloud
In an inhuman strain

Only faceless things
As calm as they come
Thinking in geometric terms
But otherwise stone dumb

di Chirico painter of sound
And silence
In worlds with neither love nor pain
Metaphysically bound
To renounce violence

Francis Bacon

Caught in the windowless deadly scarlet room
Of bare existence.
The bilious boneless male ejaculates
At some expense.

The cardinal behind his private glass
Practises screaming.

Horror the painter says is all our ration
The rest's just seeming.

Even innocent quadrupeds are caught
Naked in the bog
Of being, staring out in apprehension
Much like Goya's dog.

Christiane Kubrick

Do not miss her!

'Views from the Kitchen'
'Summer Garden with Melissa'
'Yellow Lilies in the Stable' –
All these traditional –
A woman sitting at her table –
Yet something more,
A vivid colour range –
'Bluebells and Rabbit Hole' –
Creating something rich and strange
Into a wrapt ripe contemplation
Even a chocolate Swiss roll –
Belladonna and carnation –
Here's richness of mind and soul.

Meanwhile, in other quarters of the house,
Dr Strangelove is in preparation.

Bill Viola

Pardon, mais ici un conte:

My wife was alive and we were twain.
We went into the cathedral at Nantes
And found a sort of video showing.
Reluctantly we seated ourselves
To work out what was going on.
We were gripped and watched again.
Then once again.
This was Viola's early *Triptych*
We viewed without knowing.

*

Viola's 'altarpiece' has on its central screen
A man who struggles in the water
Flanked on one side (smaller screen)
by a woman struggling to give birth,
while on the other is a tousled head:
Viola's mother struggling with her death.

These are the misty mesmerisms
Travelling continually on their loop.
Much more was to be
And could be viewed in darkness
in the National Gallery in 2003.
Faces appeared, frozen and still,
Which, if you waited there to stare
For ages of obsession,
Changed expression.

By such moments of contemplation
Comes liberation of the soul,
Viola says. We change our orientation.
Is this all hokum? My decision
Derives from watching, on the whole,
People who at the exhibition,
Standing in the dark to stare,
Experienced a wakening of religion,
Passive as if in prayer.

'He Used to Notice Such Things'

With my holly tree freshly sawn
I stood thinking, as ever I do.

A hedgehog was crossing the lawn;
Had it moods of contentment or dismay,
Did it consider when day was through
There's tomorrow, would you say?

And what of its mother,
What of worms and stars and delight
And concerns of one thing or another?
Was it all right?

Was it aware enough to enjoy or to mourn
It was only a hedgehog, crossing a lawn?

Kingsley Amis, 31 October 1995

The church is cold, as churches should be,
Cold with mortality and God's good sense.
So some of us have fortified
Ourselves beforehand. This could be
A heavy duty on the whole . . .
'Let us pray now for the soul –'
The parson makes a reference
To Jesus, crucified. Poor sod, he
Never knew our friend, who lately died.

  Time, illness, and white hair –
  For them give thanks in prayer!

Half-drowned out by the organ's blast,
In unaccustomed black, we try to sing.
'O God, our help in ages past,
Our hope –' But which of us believes a jot
Of all those pieties? They're everything –
Including God – he always mocks
In every book he wrote.
I wish the congregation here had got
Not hymn sheets but a Table d'Hôte,
Bottles not flowers to crown his lonely box.

'Time like an ever-rolling stream
Bears all –' Ah, there's a truth defined
At any rate, no matter how inaccurate
That hymned analogy may seem
To men of scientific mind.

  Time, illness, and white hair –
  For them give thanks in prayer?

'Amen.' It's over now. And we
Leave Kingsley in his coffin there,
Turn our backs, to drift off in
Our unaccustomed black –
Some for a drink, and some for two or three.

A Child's Guide to the End of the World

Deep down in the jungles and swamps lives this Stone
Age tribe. They're unsanitary, indolent, and all alone,
Bothering no one and living on fish.
Though the Golden-Eared Toad is their favourite dish.

Far off in the city, a far different kind of a tribe
Lives on champagne and tax-dodge and payback and bribe.
They've just swung the deal that the Stone Agers feared
To buy up the jungle and have it all cleared,
To pollute all the rivers, build brothels, and ruin the soil –
For a patriot's duty's to wreck all the landscape for oil.
The President smiles as he signs, for he's making a load
Of cash, plus a statue and wondrous abode.

For the jungle tribe it's the end of the road
Of course – and farewell to the Golden-Eared Toad!

At the Caligula Hotel

The dew is on the leaf, darling,
     And they are playing Ravel's *Bolero.*

'How can one endure nights without music?'
     She asks; but we are being precious.
'Oh, darling,' – sighs in the ineffectual
     Moonlight – 'how hungry I am . . .'
More caresses, or a chicken dansak?
     Like many a heart-mad lover, I
Settle for the lesser thing.
     After all, the lady's always willing,
While even Indian restaurants close
     At midnight, moon or no moon.

The dew is on the leaf
     And they are playing Ravel's *Bolero.*

     Sweet is the music of a breaking papadum.

The Roof of the World

All the joy of life is drained
Just when I was able to savour it.
Just when the brimming cup
        Just when
It reached my lips.
Just when my lips were ready.

At sunset the enemy came across the Oxus
Armed and ragged as a crow.
        With its great noise it came
Out of the eye of sunset furiously
Riding like a great barbed animal
        Many legged.

Our village burned. Flames ate the sunset.
Women were defiled
                        Children killed
I among the men taken captive.
The blood that smothered me was
        my mother's blood.
The men the enemy humiliated
The men who cursed themselves
The men the enemy humiliated
Cursed and bound and led away
Or sometimes shot.

Looking back, I saw some dotards left behind
By ruined huts and a burning donkey.
        Saw their frightened eyes
Their arms hung by their sides.
        Only that morning
That very morning on God's earth
Had they woken to bread and peace
Bread soaked in milk for their old mouths.
        Now they would weep sink down
                Curse pray die.

We captives did not speak to each other.
In silence hiding something
        In silence trying to conceal
        Something of our disgrace.
Only when night crawled dark across the plain
Starlight brought a still breeze
        A reminder of frailty
And man's insignificance
Were we allowed to halt and fall.
        Fall upon our knees
                Upon our backs
                Fall on our faces
        Die weep piss.

A great coming and going by torchlight.
        By torchlight herds of savage men
        And half-tamed animals,
                Camels roaring
        Wild mouldering smells of ordure
                And cooking
All dark even in flickering light
        Fighting and cries and laughter
        As from a distant place and age.

Scraps were thrown to us
        Gristle and crust and bone.
For which we fought like dogs
        Like jackals in the dust.

Sleeping still tied
Our souls were bound
        Even in sleep
In the midst of our foetid sleep
In the midst of the night's foul sleep
Under mist under moon
Cries and animal grunts
        For the corpse of the past.

Before dawn dragged its crayon to the eastern sky
Or chill of first light stirred our bones
The horde rose up
      All shadowy the hated horde
         Cursed and rose up
And kicked their steeds onto their feet.
They started on another day
      With stale *nan* between their teeth
And perforce we followed
With our stale nightmares.

We followed on by woven rope
We followed on by woven hemp
We followed on by force
We swallowed dust, choked on stale *roti*
Followed on.
The sun rose up and swallowed everything.
We followed growing weaker every day
      While reds and greens lit shadows at our feet
      And grey ticks bred into our eyes and mouths.

The savage men were married to their mares
Though some had women at their back.
Some copulated as they rode
And all relieved themselves
      Upon the hoof

Their urine
Trailing backwards like a tinselled rein
Soaking Tajikistan.
Their language was not ours
      Their tongues had different roots
      Their speech carried a bitter herb
      Their lips curled to a sullen tune.
Their look was more opaque
      Blind as a stone.
Their females had mud in their cheeks
And vaginal decay with their aromas.
Their banners flew like muddied oaths.
        If they had gods

Things to bow down at
Those gods were blind and carved from malachite
        And poisonous as crabs.
Their dress was of a different kind
        Stinking and leatherous
        Cut from the hides of horses.
Only their lances were pure
        Like splinters of the sun.

When darkness in its cloak
    Clothed all of us below
The great distant mountains
Stood sugar pink with light.
There lived the wicked gods
    Thunder their laughter
Who saw when we ate grubs
    Maggots, grasshoppers
Beetles that burned our cheeks.

When one of our number died
        When he could go no more
        When the rope about his neck choked him
        When his spirit left him on the march
When he fell like a rotten prop
Then was he cut free.
It needed but one slash
The carcass left behind

For the kite hawks and flies
        And obscene things
For the sun and wind to empty
        Peck clean that dirty object
Bedded in the dust.
None of us looked behind.

A hollow had been carved in barren ground
A bowl where soil had been
With something like a ragged stream.
By this stream we came upon
        A starved assembly of animals
            Their noses in the muddied water
Their riders in repose smoking grass.
Their ragged women baking
        Unleavened bread on hot stones.

Prisoners like us
        As ragged and ashamed as we
Stood among dwarf trees
Staring with white eyes
        At the bruised purple sky.
By their aspect we understood
        Nothing needed to be said.
Theirs was a long captivity.

Captivity? But then a rifle cracked
        And one fell free
Twitching and then was still.
From these sawdust men we learnt
A truth undrinkable as brine.
The conditions under which
We might regain
        If we could live that long
                Our liberty
It all depended on the capital
        And rich men in the capital.
It all depended if the capital
Would pay a ransom
        Would pay our weight in gold.

We looked askance
        At one another
                Without speech
Saying *Who in the city*
Would have an interest in such as us?
Would dream of paying one dinar,
Would dream of forfeiting
                A cent
For desert tribes like us?

I sat a little way
I sat a little way apart
I sat apart
From those other unfortunates,
Wondering would I see
        Would I ever see
My home and her I loved?
        Yes, she! Her I loved
Above the mysterious moon
Her dear dark eyes
        Her mouth
                See again
And why should cruel fate
Treat anyone this way?

But this is how it was
In our Tajikistan
Under the high Pamirs
The Roof of the World.

The Red Pavilion

Winding paths lead to the waterfall.
By a clump of bamboo lies my pool.
Koi are fed by crumbs from my hand.
One slow tortoise is permitted.
The little hill is planted
With suitable trees
To make the landscape mild but safe.
The object of my garden is
To improve on Nature.

Through the sallow afternoon
Through a stand of silver birch
The red pavilion
Where doves coo in the eaves
A place of rest and solitude
Soon White Lotus will arrive
Bringing wine in my bronze jug
With quiet companionship
An insipid life is to be preferred.

About the Author

Brian Aldiss has enjoyed a long, remarkable career as a distinguished and prolific author of science fiction. However, in addition to writing classics of the genre such as *Hothouse*, *Non-Stop* and the *Helliconia* series, he is known as an important mainstream novelist, poet, essayist, dramatist and critic. He has also written extensively on visual art and created numerous abstract works of his own.

Born in Dereham, Norfolk, in 1925, Aldiss began writing stories, which his mother bound in pieces of wallpaper, from the age of three. In a series of boarding schools, the young Brian honed his natural talent as a storyteller after lights out. Serving in the Army from 1943–47, he was stationed in India, Assam, Burma, Sumatra, Singapore and Hong Kong, and these wartime experiences would later provide material for a number of books, both dismaying and humorous.

After the War, Aldiss settled in Oxford, where he began to work as a bookseller while selling stories and articles to magazines and attracting the attention of publishers. *The Brightfount Diaries*, his first novel, was published in 1956 and was followed by a collection of science-fiction stories, *Space, Time and Nathaniel*, in the following year. He is now the author of over sixty books that have been widely translated and published across the world, and his life as a writer has provided him with many opportunities to travel. He is twice married and now Lady A is his constant companion. They have many friends in the USA.

A Fellow of the Royal Society of Literature, Aldiss has won and been nominated for numerous international awards, including the Hugo Best Short Story, the Prix Jules Verne, the British Science Fiction Award and the J. Lloyd Eaton Memorial Award. In 2000 he was elected Grand Master by the Science Fiction Writers of America and in 2005 received an OBE for Service to Literature.